This book belongs to

_____

_____

_____

For Doris and George
—A.H.B.

For Matthew and Sally
—J.C.

tiger tales
an imprint of ME Media, LLC
202 Old Ridgefield Road, Wilton, CT 06897
Originally published in the United States as *What If?* by Little Tiger Press 1996
This paperback edition published in the United States 2003
Originally published in Great Britain 1996 by Little Tiger Press
An imprint of Magi Publications
Text ©1996 A.H. Benjamin
Illustrations ©1996 Jane Chapman
CIP data is available
ISBN 1-58925-381-7
Printed in Singapore

BAA! MOO!
WHAT WILL WE DO?

by
A.H. BENJAMIN

Illustrated by
JANE CHAPMAN

tiger tales

Something special was about to happen at Buttercup Farm. The farmer had brought a kangaroo back with him from Australia. She was going to arrive that day! All the animals gathered in the barnyard to talk about it. No one had ever seen a kangaroo before.

"What can a kangaroo do,
anyway?" everyone wanted
to know.

"What if she can crow?" said Rooster. "What if she gets up very early and crows very loudly, and wakes up the whole farm? And what if she counts the chickens and hens to see if any are missing? If she does all that, the farmer won't need me anymore. I'll have to look for a new job!

Cock-a-doodle-do!

What if I can't find another job?"

"How terrible!"
everyone said.

"What if she can herd sheep?" asked Dog. "What if she rounds them all up and takes them out to graze in the field? And what if she chases foxes, too? The farmer will be so happy with her that he'll send me off to live someplace else.

Bow-wow!

I would hate to leave!"

"It would be horrible!"

everyone agreed.

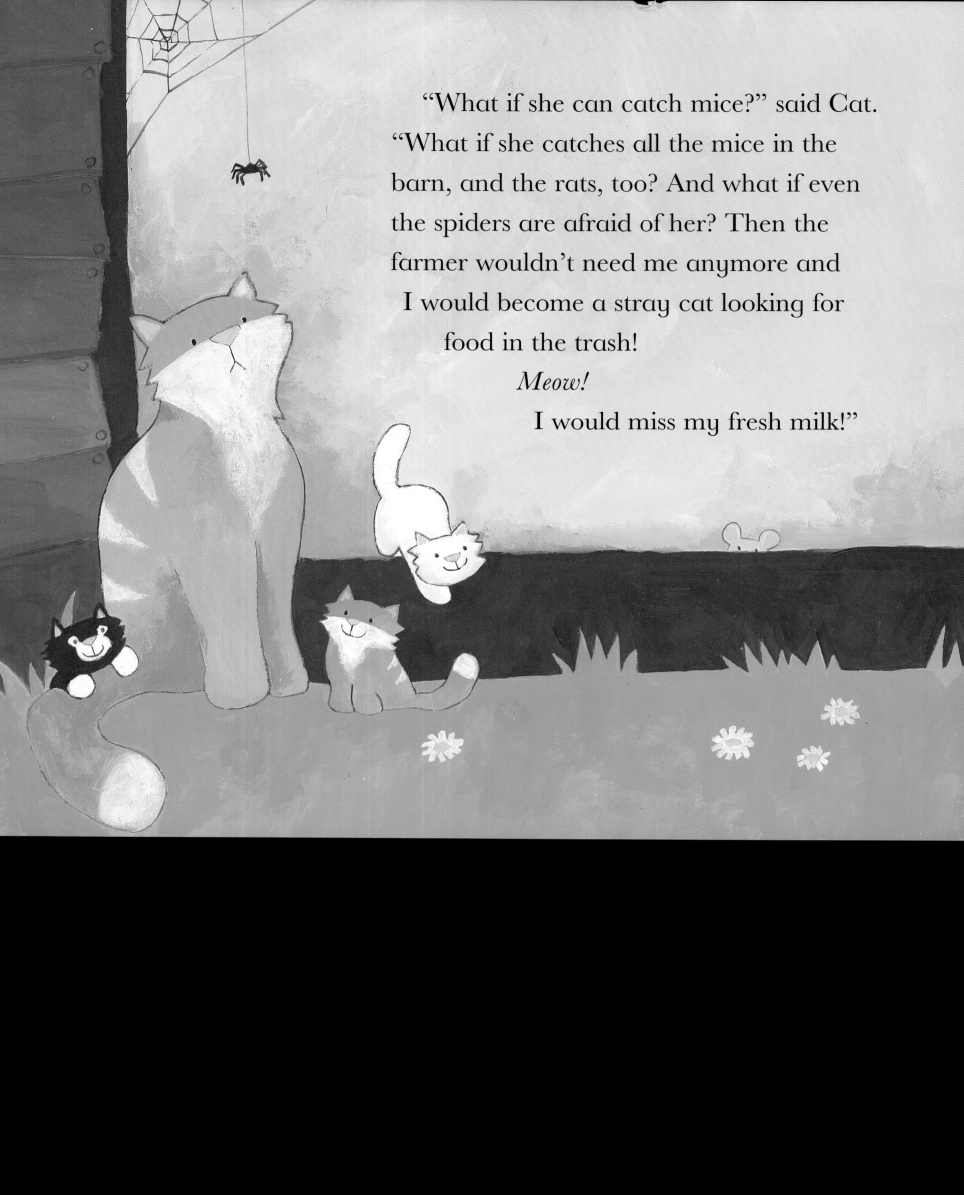

"What if she can catch mice?" said Cat. "What if she catches all the mice in the barn, and the rats, too? And what if even the spiders are afraid of her? Then the farmer wouldn't need me anymore and I would become a stray cat looking for food in the trash!

Meow!

I would miss my fresh milk!"

"How awful!"
said everyone.

"What if she gives milk?" asked Cow. "What if she fills up all the buckets in the barn with such creamy milk that people will rush to buy it? Then nobody would want my milk, and I'd have to pull the heavy plough through the field instead.

Moo!

I couldn't stand that!"

"How Shocking!"

everyone said.

"What if she grows wool?" said Sheep.
"What if she has a thick, woolly fleece, softer
and whiter than mine? And what if her wool
grows twice as fast as mine? The farmer would
be so happy with her that he'd only use my
wool for rags, instead of nice sweaters.

Baa!

I don't want my wool used for rags!"

"It would be terrible!"
everyone agreed.

"What if she can pull a cart?" said Horse. "What if she takes a cartful of fruit and vegetables to the market faster than I do? And what if she gives rides to the farmer's children? There would be no place here for me then, and I'd end up in the stable with all the old horses!

Neigh!

I'm too young to live in that old stable!"

"How frightening!"

said everyone.

The animals were getting worried. They were
so busy worrying they didn't notice that some of
the younger animals had wandered away.
"Where are my puppies?" asked Dog.

"And my kittens?" said Cat.
Sheep couldn't find her lamb, either.

The animals searched all over
the place, but not a kitten, puppy,
or lamb was in sight.
They looked from the barn . . .

to the pigsty, with no luck.

"This is horrible!" crowed Rooster.

"Terrible!" barked Dog.

"Awful!" meowed Cat.

"Shocking!" mooed Cow.

"Frightening!" baaed Sheep.

"This is very bad," neighed Horse.

Suddenly, across the field they saw . . .

a very strange animal, leaping
and jumping toward them.

"Hello!" she said.
"I'm Kangaroo!"

The animals stopped searching for their children. They stared at Kangaroo. This new animal had a large pouch on her stomach, and in the pouch . . .

were three kittens,
two puppies,
and one lamb!

"I've found your babies," said Kangaroo. "I'm a baby-sitter. I look after the children, and give them a ride in my pouch when they get tired. They love it!"

"What a great idea!" the animals cried. And crowing and barking and meowing and mooing and baaing and neighing, they all welcomed Kangaroo to Buttercup Farm.

Laura's Star
by Klaus Baumgart
ISBN 1-58925-374-4

Pedro the Brave
by Leo Broadley
illustrated by Holly Swain
ISBN 1-58925-375-2

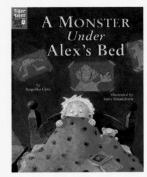

A Monster Under Alex's Bed
by Angelika Glitz
illustrated by Imke Sönnichsen
ISBN 1-58925-373-6

Explore the world of tiger tales!

More fun-filled and exciting stories await you!
Look for these titles and more at your local library or bookstore.
And have fun reading!

tiger tales

202 Old Ridgefield Road, Wilton, CT 06897

The Very Lazy Ladybug
by Isobel Finn
illustrated by Jack Tickle
ISBN 1-58925-379-5

Snarlyhissopus
by Alan MacDonald
illustrated by Louise Voce
ISBN 1-58925-370-1

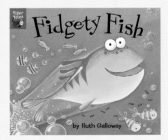

Fidgety Fish
by Ruth Galloway
ISBN 1-58925-377-9